PIXAR ANIMATION STUDIOS

ARTIST SHOWCASE

BOX meets Circle

Aaron Hartline

Disney Press

Los Angeles • New York

Hello, my name
is Box.

I'm
Circle!

We should
do something
together.

I know...

Little jumps.

Big
jumps!

Up
and
down.

All
around.

I can't jump.

Every time I try...

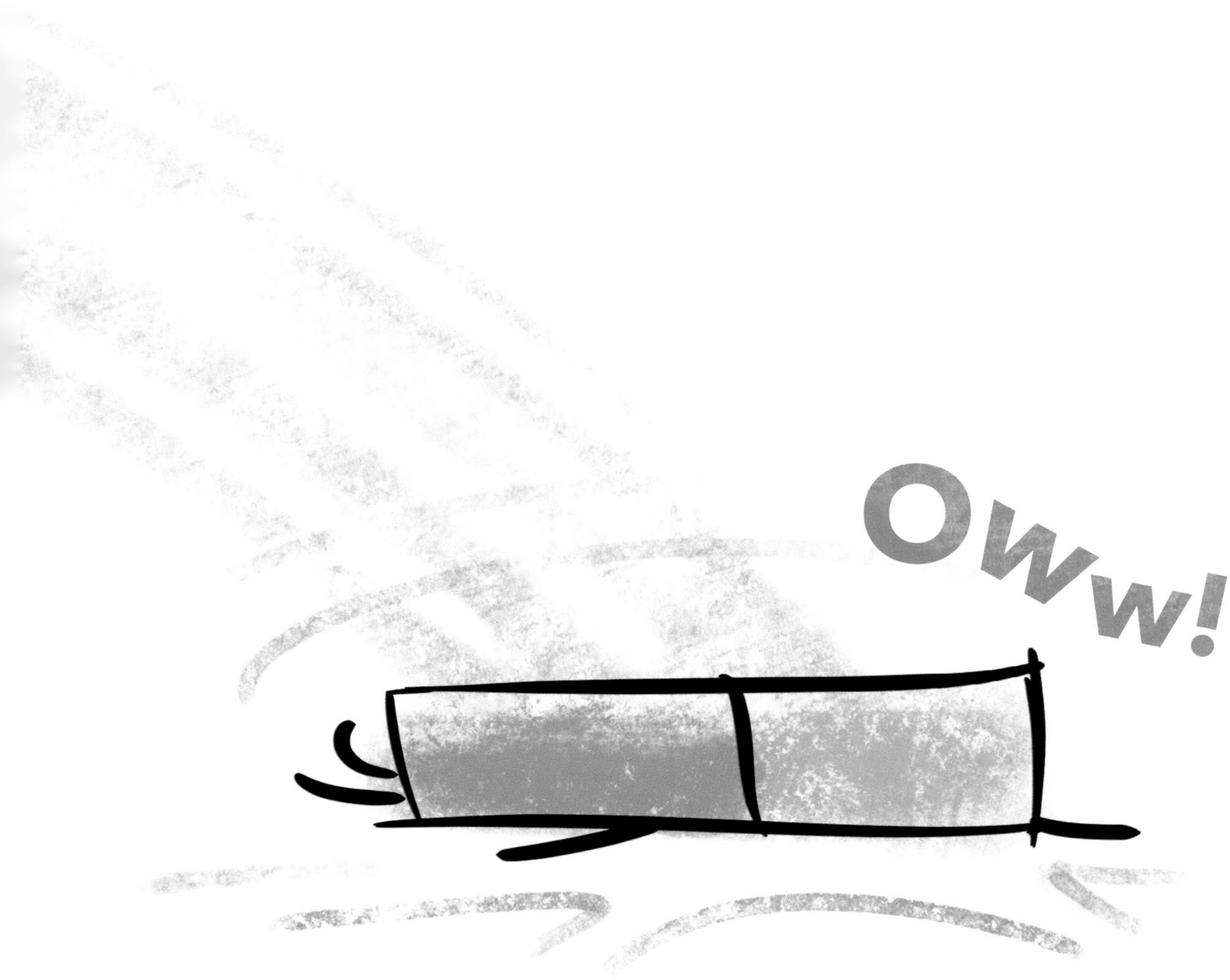
Oww!

I know!

Let's **sit!**

Suntanning.

Snuggling.

Playing games.

Doing homework.

ERR, never mind.

Sitting is the best!

Like this?

can't...

The
End

I just need to sit—
and think of an idea.

That's it!

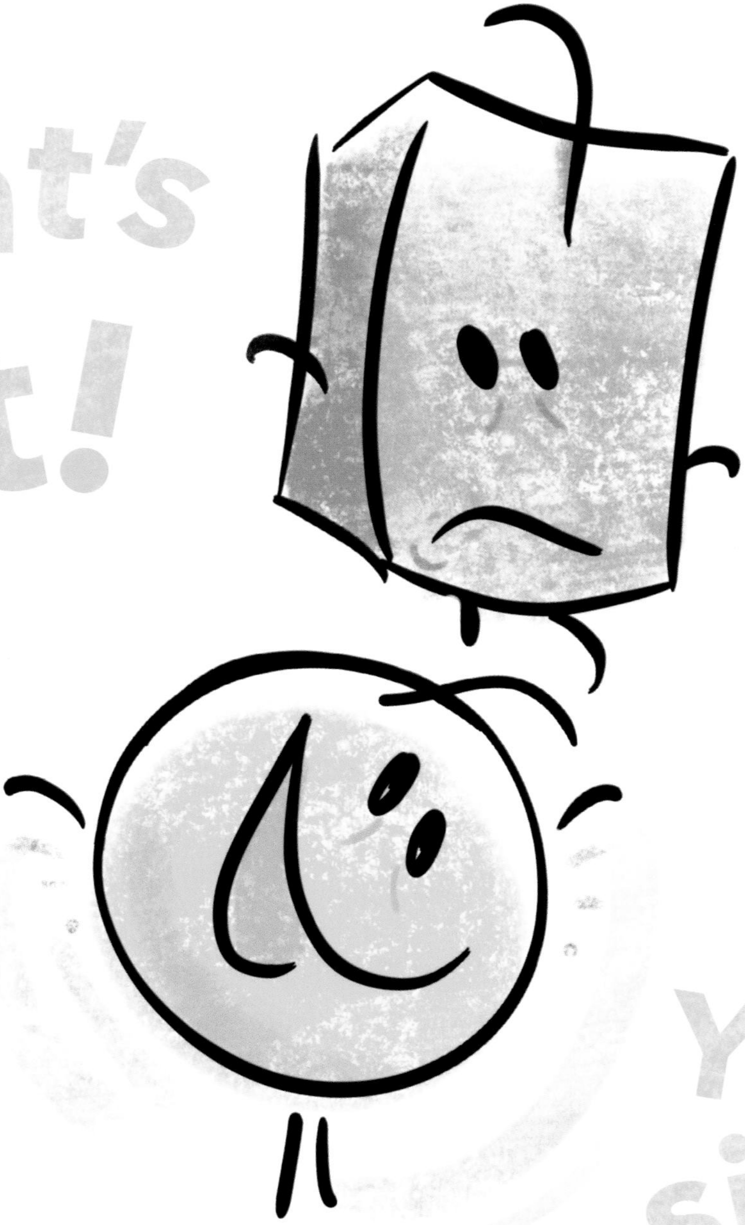

You sit...

...and you JUMP!

We found something

we can do together!

Hi, I'm Aaron!

When I was a kid, I loved two things: drawing and movies. So when I discovered animation, I was thrilled to have found a career that combines these two passions.

When I saw Buzz and Woody for the first time in *Toy Story*, I realized I didn't want to be just any animator; I wanted to be a Pixar animator.

But it didn't happen right away. Year after year, for thirteen years, I applied but didn't get in.

Rather than give up, I continued to work hard and get better at my craft.

In 2008, it finally happened: I was offered a job at Pixar.

Since then, I have worked on films like *Up*, *Toy Story 3*, and *Inside Out*.

Working at Pixar is a dream come true for me.

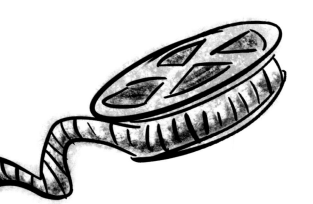

Animation at Pixar happens on
computers, but, like I said,
I've always loved to draw. I especially
enjoy quick, simple doodles.

Now, thanks to the
Pixar Artist Showcase,
I can share these adventures with
you and your family!

That's how Box and Circle appeared.
I would sketch out their
little adventures
and enjoy reading them
with my family.

About the Pixar Animation Studios Artist Showcase

This series of original picture books puts the spotlight on the incredible artists of Pixar Animation Studios. The pages of each book showcase the personal work of one of these talented artists and introduce a brand-new world and characters.

For my family, Karen, Jackson, and Autumn

Published by Disney Press, an imprint of Disney Book Group.

No part of this book may be reproduced or transmitted in any form or by any means, electronic or mechanical, including photocopying, recording, or by any information storage and retrieval system, without written permission from the publisher. For information address Disney Press, 1101 Flower Street, Glendale, California 91201.

Printed in Malaysia

First Hardcover Edition, April 2018

1 3 5 7 9 10 8 6 4 2

FAC-029191-18005

Designed by Aaron Hartline and Scott Piehl

Reinforced binding

Library of Congress Cataloging-in-Publication Data

Names: Hartline, Aaron, author, illustrator.

Title: Box meets Circle / Aaron Hartline.

Description: First edition. Los Angeles ; New York : Disney Press, 2018.

Series: Walt Disney Animation Studios Artist Showcase Summary: "Circle likes to jump, but Box can't jump. Box likes to sit. Will they ever find a way to play together?" –Provided by publisher.

Identifiers: LCCN 2017031501 (print) LCCN 2017043406 (ebook)

ISBN 9781368020718 (ebook) ISBN 9781368015875 (hardcover)

Subjects: CYAC: Individuality-Fiction. Friendship-Fiction. Boxes-Fiction. Circle-Fiction.

Classification: LCC PZ7.1.H3765 (ebook) LCC PZ7.1.H3765 Box 2018 (print)

DDC [E]-dc23

LC record available at https://lccn.loc.gov/2017031501

ISBN 978-1-368-01587-5

Visit www.disneybooks.com